The Chocolate Unicorn

JENNY McLACHLAN

ILLUSTRATED BY SARAH LAWRENCE

BLOOMSBURY EDUCATION
Bloomsbury Publishing Plc
50 Bedford Square, London, WC1B 3DP, UK

BLOOMSBURY, BLOOMSBURY EDUCATION and the Diana logo
are trademarks of Bloomsbury Publishing Plc

First published in Great Britain in 2020 by Bloomsbury Publishing Plc

A catalogue record for this book is available from the British Library

ISBN: PB: 978-1-4729-7262-0; ePDF: 978-1-4729-7263-7; ePub: 978-1-4729-7261-3;
enhanced ePub: 978-1-4729-7260-6

2 4 6 8 10 9 7 5 3 1

Printed and bound in India by Replika Press Pvt. Ltd.

All papers used by Bloomsbury Publishing Plc are natural, recyclable products from wood grown
in well managed forests and other controlled material.

To find out more about our authors and books visit www.bloomsbury.com
and sign up for our newsletters

Chapter One

Olive Brown was a bit of a worrier. When Olive went to a birthday party, she never went on the bouncy castle. What if she got bounced too high?

When Olive met a sunbathing cat, she never stroked it. What if it scratched her?

When Olive felt like dressing up as a pirate and walking to her grandpa's house, she *just didn't*. What if someone saw her?

What Olive Brown needed was some courage, but what she got was a box of chocolates. They were a present from Grandpa, and written on the front were the words 'A Little Box of Magic'.

A Little Box of Magic

When Olive opened
the box, she found:

a chocolate fairy
with a popping
candy wand,

a chocolate
troll with a
coconut nose,

a chocolate elf with
a striped toffee hat,

a chocolate
mermaid with a
marshmallow tail,

a chocolate dragon
with marzipan scales,

and, best of all, a chocolate unicorn
with fudge hooves and a glittery horn.

A Little Box
of Magic

Olive had never seen anything that looked so beautiful (or delicious) in her life. She decided to eat the chocolates one at a time to make them last as long as possible.

On Monday she ate the elf
(his hat tasted minty).

On Tuesday she ate the mermaid
(her tail tasted of lemons).

The fairy, troll and dragon were gobbled up by the weekend, but Olive couldn't eat the chocolate unicorn. He was too magical.

Every night and every morning, Olive looked at the chocolate unicorn, but she never took a bite.

Chapter Two

Then, one day, Olive opened her box of chocolates and the chocolate unicorn had vanished!
Before Olive could even begin to worry, she spotted some fudgy hoof prints.

They led across the bedside table, over the duvet cover and under the bed. When Olive pulled up the duvet, she couldn't believe her eyes. There was the chocolate unicorn exploring her craft box.

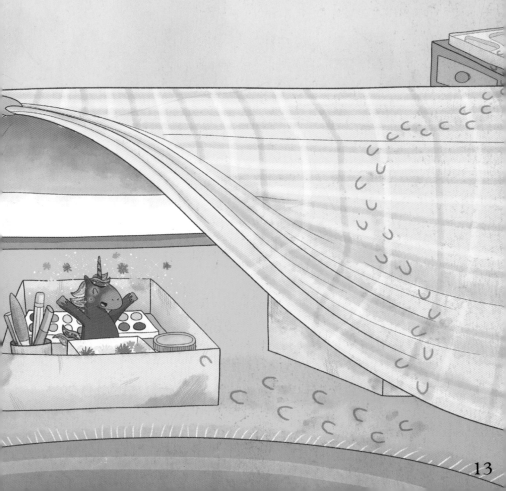

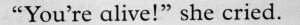
"You're alive!" she cried.

"Well I had to do something," said
the chocolate unicorn. "I was getting
bored stuck in that box of chocolates!"
Then he galloped out of the room
leaving a trail of glitter behind him.

Olive followed the chocolate unicorn down the stairs and out into the garden. "What is *that*?" said the chocolate unicorn. He was gazing at the neighbour's cat who was lying asleep on the grass.

"That's Ginger and he's a cat,"
said Olive.
"He's so fluffy!" cried the chocolate
unicorn, then he ran across the grass
and started rolling around on Ginger's
tummy.

Ginger's eyes pinged open and he
licked his lips greedily.
Olive rushed forwards, scooped up the
chocolate unicorn and popped him
in her pocket. "Good cat," she said,
stroking Ginger's soft fur.

Just then, Mum came outside. She blinked with surprise when she saw Olive stroking Ginger.
"I thought you were scared of cats," she said.
"The chocolate unicorn made me do it!" said Olive.

Chapter Three

That afternoon, Olive went to a summer fair with her mum. She took the chocolate unicorn with her to keep him out of trouble. They were watching a magic show when the magician asked for a volunteer.

"Oooh, me, me!" cried the chocolate unicorn, and he leapt off Olive's lap and galloped towards the stage. Olive chased after him.

"It looks like we have our volunteer!"
said the magician, putting a top hat
on Olive's head.

When Olive got back to her seat, Mum said, "That was brave!"
"The chocolate unicorn made me do it," whispered Olive.

Chapter Four

The next day, Olive and the chocolate unicorn walked to the park. They played in the sandpit and the chocolate unicorn found a dropped ice cream.

The chocolate unicorn was trotting round the pond when he spotted a bird in a tree. "What is *that*?" he said. "It's a parakeet," said Olive.

"It's *so* green. Let's go and look at it!" said the chocolate unicorn, then he dashed across the grass and scrambled up the tree.

Olive didn't know what to do. She had never climbed a tree before. What if she got stuck? But if the chocolate unicorn could do it then so could she! Olive grabbed a branch and began to climb.

Olive discovered it was wonderful hiding
in the leaves at the top of the tree. She
sat with the chocolate unicorn watching
the parakeet until it flew away. Then
they spied on all the people in the park.
"I feel like I'm a giant," said Olive.

"Olive?" Mum was smiling and peering up through the leaves. "What are you doing up there? Did the chocolate unicorn make you do it?"

"Yes," said Olive, "but it was a bit of me too!"

Chapter Five

Olive took the chocolate unicorn everywhere she went.

The chocolate unicorn loved trying new things, so Olive tried new things too. They walked to Grandpa's house dressed as pirates and did a dance for him *in the front garden*.

They let snails slither over them and
rolled down a steep hill. They even
went on a bouncy castle together and
bounced too high.

Olive discovered that the more things she tried, the braver she became. Then Olive took the chocolate unicorn to the seaside.

They explored the rock pools and collected shells.

When the chocolate unicorn saw a boy making a sandcastle his eyes grew wide. "I'd *love* to do that," he said. "Let's help!"

"What if he doesn't want us to?" said Olive.
"There's only one way to find out," said
the chocolate unicorn. "Let's ask him."
So Olive walked over to the boy and said,
"Please can we play with you?"

The boy looked up, smiled, then passed her a bucket. His name was Eric (it said so on his t-shirt). He didn't talk to Olive, but they still built an amazing sandcastle together.

Olive was digging the moat, when Mum asked if she wanted to come for a swim. "Do you want to come in the sea, Eric?" said Olive.

Eric looked at the tumbling waves and screaming children and shook his head. Olive understood. Usually she paddled at the edge of the water, too scared of the noise and the waves to go any further.

But today she felt different. Today, she
felt brave.

"Will you come in the sea?" she asked
the chocolate unicorn.

"I can't," he said sadly. "It's too wet
for me. I'd go gloopy."

He was right. The sea was no place for a chocolate unicorn, but it was just the place for Olive. So she left him with Eric and ran towards the sea.

A big wave got Olive right in the face. It knocked her down and Mum pulled her up again. She screamed as she jumped over waves and as waves jumped over her.

It was so much fun that Olive stayed in the sea until her fingers were wrinkly and she was shivering with cold.

As they walked up the beach, Mum
said, "I suppose the chocolate unicorn
made you do that?"
"No, it was all me!" laughed Olive.

Chapter Six

Back at the sandcastle, Olive found
Eric chatting away to the chocolate
unicorn. He stopped talking as soon as
he saw Olive.
"You can play with him if you want,"
said Olive.

Eric smiled and built the chocolate
unicorn a sandy cave to keep him out
of the sun.

Together, they made the sandcastle
bigger and bigger until
Eric's dad said it was
time to go home.

As Eric packed up his buckets and
spades, Olive said to the chocolate
unicorn, "I've been thinking. Would
you like to go home with Eric? I think
he's shy, but he'd love talking to you."

"That would be fun," said the
chocolate unicorn, then he looked sad.
"But I think I will miss you, Olive!"
"I will miss you too," said Olive, "but I
will never, ever forget you."

Olive kissed the chocolate unicorn on the end of his nose and put him in Eric's bucket. She wanted him to be a surprise.

Then she ran across the sand towards the sparkling sea.

As Olive leapt over the first wave, she smiled. She was thinking about all the adventures Eric and the chocolate unicorn would have together.

Olive had found her courage. Now it was Eric's turn.

And maybe next summer they would be jumping over the waves together!